OWEN HAS BURGERS AND DRUM

Helping to Understand and Befriend Kids with Asperger's Syndrome

by Christine M. Sheils with Frank R. Pane, MAE, BCBA
illustrated by Anita DuFalla

New Horizon Press
Far Hills, New Jersey

Dedication

Dedicated to the hope of building understanding
and acceptance for every child.
— CMS

I would like to dedicate this book to all the families and children
with whom I have worked. May they continue to reach their goals.
— FRP

Copyright © 2013 by Christine M. Sheils with Frank R. Pane, MAE, BCBA
Illustrations by Anita DuFalla

Requests for permission should be addressed to:
New Horizon Press
P.O. Box 669
Far Hills, NJ 07931

Christine M. Sheils with Frank R. Pane, MAE, BCBA
Owen Has Burgers and Drum:
    Helping to Understand and Befriend Kids with Asperger's Syndrome

Cover Design and Illustrations: Anita DuFalla
Interior Design: Charley Nasta

Library of Congress Control Number: 2012945208
ISBN 13: 978-0-88282-434-5

SMALL HORIZONS
A Division of New Horizon Press

2017 2016 2015 2014 2013   1 2 3 4 5

Printed in the U.S.A.

Mr. Henderson
Vice Principal

Down the hallway I raced like a baseball player stealing second base. Up the ramp and around the corner… almost there…my feet pounded on top of shiny white tile, perfect for the sliding **swoosh** into the classroom. I was sure to be first today.

"Whoa, slow down, Calvin!" Vice Principal Henderson bellowed. I smiled at him from beneath my eyebrows and walked the last few steps to my classroom.

I slipped inside and looked around. "YESSSSS, FIRST!" I whispered, pumping my fist in the air. That was when I heard it.

"Owen...HAS burgers and drum."

What does that mean? I wondered.

The woman who had spoken stood near my classroom door. She had long black hair. I realized I had seen her before.

Her family had just moved next door and my mom said they had a boy named Owen who was seven years old, just like me.

Yesterday I had watched from my bedroom window as she talked to my mom. I was hoping to meet Owen or at least to see him.

"Good morning, Calvin," my teacher, Mrs. Gilson, said. "I thought you and Owen could sit together."

"Uh...sure," I stammered.

Then I saw him. Owen stood smiling in the doorway, staring into the classroom. He was taller than I was with thick, black hair neatly combed. I liked the cool Saturn T-shirt he wore. He was pulling one of those wheelie backpacks.

Hmmm....no burgers or drum, I thought as he walked in. *UNLESS...they are in his backpack!*

"Hi, Owen, my name is Cal," I said when he sat down next to me. "I live next door to you." I could not wait to ask him about the burgers and drum.

He stared straight ahead. Then a smile came over his face and his eyes got as big as frisbees. "Pluto is not a REAL planet," he said. "It is a dwarf planet. It takes 248 years to orbit the sun."

He was grinning widely now, his big round eyes darting at me and everywhere else.

"Cool!" I replied.

"There are eight planets in our solar system," he added. "Not nine."

Clap...clap...clap, clap, clap.

I could tell Owen wanted to say more, but Mrs. Gilson's clapping hands stopped him.

"Boys and girls," Mrs. Gilson said, nodding at Owen, "this is Owen. He is joining our class today. He has moved all the way from California."

Forty-six eyeballs looked our way.

Owen sat in his seat and began to take out pieces of paper and stick them on his desk. When I whispered, "What are you doing?" Owen said, "I am reading the teacher's rules." He studied them carefully, then stared straight ahead.

"Calvin," Mrs. Gilson asked me just before center time, "could you help Owen read a book at centers today? Show him how it is done." She winked.

I waved to Owen. "Come on, Owen, we can read together. It is buddy reading."

We sat down by the bookshelves in the corner of the room. "Hey, Owen, do you play T-ball?" I still wanted to ask him about the burgers and drum.

"DO YOU LIKE MY NEW SHIRT?" Owen shouted. "IT IS A SATURN SHIRT!"

His eyes stared at me, then quickly shifted away.

"Yes, it is cool." I really DID like his shirt. I waited for Owen to say more, but he was silent.

I grabbed a book off the shelf and held it up. "How about this one, Owen?" He still did not say anything. "It is my favorite," I added. Owen did not even glance at the book.

I turned to the first page and began to read out loud. When it was Owen's turn to read, he was looking over his shoulder and out the window.

I nudged him and pointed to the place where I had left off, but Owen kept looking out the window.

"Maybe he is looking for Pluto," one boy snickered.

"Hey, Owen," I asked at recess. "Do you want to play soccer?" He smiled a big, toothy grin. Then he snatched the ball out of my hands and ran away.

"Owen, STOP!" I yelled.

"GIVE ME BACK THE BALL!"

Owen did not stop. He kept running and laughing like he did not hear me or worse, did not care.

I gave him an angry look when we were back inside…and he smiled at me…again! What is UP with this dude? Doesn't he know I am ANGRY with him?

"Calvin…Calvin?" It was Mrs. Gilson. "Could you please read your story to the class?"

Everyone laughed when I read *Mr. Monkey Goes Bananas*, even Mrs. Gilson.

I was starting to forget about what happened at recess. Suddenly Owen shouted, "I LIKE YOU, CAL!"

My eyes opened wide and my face got hot.

"Look, he is turning red!" Andrew scoffed. "He looks like Mister Tomato Head."

I wanted to hide under my desk.

That night, just before bedtime, I told my mom about Owen. "I heard his mom say something weird: 'He has burgers and drum.' What is that?"

My mom's eyebrows scrunched together and her forehead got wrinkly. She nodded slowly and smiled.

"I think you heard his mom say 'Asperger's syndrome,' not 'has burgers and drum.' That is a challenge Owen has. It is part of what is known as the *autism spectrum*. Owen is smart like you, Cal, but it is hard for him to know how to be a friend. It will take time."

"Well, okay. What about all the rules?" I groaned.

"What rules?" Mom waited for me to go on.

"He has these notes with rules on his desk," I explained. "They say stuff like: look at your teacher… sit quietly…raise your hand."

Mom was silent for a moment. Then she said, "Remember when you could not tie your shoelaces?"

"Yes."

"So I gave you that lacing book?"

"Oh, yes," I nodded.

"You kept that book on your nightstand to help you remember, right?"

"Yes, I did."

"Maybe it is like that, Cal," said Mom. "Owen just needs reminders."

"I guess," I shrugged.

She wrapped her arms around me and gave me a hug.

I watched car headlights zoom across my walls and ceiling as I lay in bed.

I did not understand it, this…as…asboo…this burgers and drum thing, but I could tell by Mom's serious voice that it was something important.

The next morning at school, Owen shouted, "HI, CAL! HOW YA DOIN', PARTNER?" He was standing so close, I could see his nose hairs!

I backed up a bit. "Hi, Owen. What's up?"

Owen just stood there like he was going to say more, but he did not. I began to realize that talking back and forth was not easy for Owen.

A few days later when I said, "What's up?" Owen said, "The sky." I was not sure if he was trying to be funny, but I laughed anyway.

"Good one, Owen," I said.

Most mornings started with Owen shouting, "How ya doin', partner?" One day I ignored him. I did not answer, because Andrew and I were hatching a plan. Boy, was that a mistake!

"May I please go get a drink?" I asked Mrs. Gilson.

"Me too?" asked Andrew.

Mrs. Gilson gave us a stern look. "Okay, boys, but come right back."

We high-fived each other outside the classroom door and headed for the long hallway with the shiny floor, perfect for practicing baseball slides. I went first.

"Awesome." Andrew whispered.

Then it was Andrew's turn. **Swoosh!**

"Safe by a mile," I told him.

"You are not supposed to be here."

We turned around. It was Owen.

Andrew got up and brushed off his pants. "Mind your own beeswax," he snapped. Then he looked at me and smirked, "It is your...ahem...BEST friend."

"It is the rule," Owen scowled.

Ugh, I thought, *Owen and his rules.*

I started back up the hallway. "It is okay, Owen," I said. "Just a couple more slides."

Suddenly, the fire alarm began to ring. We all jumped, then froze. The ringer was just above our heads.

Andrew was the first to move. "Come on, Cal!" he called. "In here." He opened a door with the letters **C L O S E T**.

"I am worried that Mrs. Gilson will notice we are missing," I said.

"We will tell her we went outside with another class. COME ON!" he yelled.

I slipped inside and closed the door. It was really dark. I felt my way along the rows of shelves and crouched down beside Andrew.

Then the door flew open. Owen's silhouette filled the doorway. "You are not supposed to be here!" Owen yelled.

Andrew elbowed me. "He is going to ruin everything!"

"It is okay, Owen!" I replied. "Just go back to class."

"YOU ARE NOT SUPPOSED TO BE HERE!" Owen shouted. He put his hands over his ears. "IT IS THE RULE!" I could tell Owen was upset and I knew it would only get worse.

"You need to come with me! You are not supposed to be here!" Owen insisted.

I turned to Andrew. "We should go," I said.

We both ran out the door and down the hallway after Owen. His hands were still over his ears to try to block the alarm bell's noise as he led the way. I remembered—he hated loud sounds.

The three of us turned the corner.

Oh my gosh! **SMOKE!** The first grade hall was filled with it.

At the end of the hallway, Owen slowed down and stopped. I guessed he was lost and not sure which way to go to get out of the building.

He would not move.

I grabbed one of Owen's arms and Andrew grabbed the other. We both pulled as hard as we could until we were all safely out the front door.

"Cool!" Owen said when he saw the fire trucks outside. Mrs. Gilson was talking to Mr. Henderson and pointing right at us.

Mr. Henderson hurried over. "Where have you boys been?"

I told Mr. Henderson everything, including the hiding part. "If it were not for Owen..." Mr. Henderson started to say.

"Yes, I know," I blurted out. I did not want to think about that. Then I looked at Owen. He was staring straight ahead.

"Thanks, partner," I said.

"Thanks, Owen," Andrew said.

Owen turned and looked at us. "It is the rule," he said.

I let out a deep sigh. For the first time, I was really glad Owen had rules and made us follow them.

I was thinking about that when Owen said loudly, "I like you, Cal. You are my BEST friend, Cal." Then he added, "I like you too, Andrew. You are also my best friend."

We both looked at Owen. He was looking right at us and smiling his big, toothy grin. This time my face did not turn red. I smiled back and so did Andrew.

"You are our best friend too, Owen," I said.

"Yes," added Andrew.

Tips for Children

1. Children with Asperger's syndrome (AS), part of the autism spectrum, may have difficulty making friends. A smile and a friendly greeting from you can be a good start.

2. A child with AS sometimes has difficulty listening to a friend. It might take him or her a little bit of time to understand what you are saying. Be patient.

3. Jokes are not always easily understood by someone with AS. Try again or tell a different joke. You may need to explain the joke.

4. Children with AS can get frustrated and might need a break.

5. A child with AS can appear to be ignoring you, because having a conversation with others may be difficult for him or her. You can help by talking and asking questions.

6. Be a model student, because children with AS sometimes have difficulty sitting quietly and paying attention.

7. A child with AS might not have a lot of interests like you. Share your interests so he or she can learn about them.

8. If someone is being mean to a child with AS, stand up for him or her.

9. AS is not contagious. You cannot get it from someone else.

10. There is no cure for AS. However, children with AS can learn and grow just like you.

Tips for Parents and Educators

- Social interactions with others, specifically peers, can be difficult for children with Asperger's syndrome (AS), which is part of the autism spectrum. Keep expectations realistic, so as to not create anxiety and stress for the child. Promote social interactions with other peers. At school, consider setting up a buddy system.

- Model ways to interact with others. Teach children with AS how to initiate conversations, such as greeting another person and then asking a question or making a comment. Also, children with AS might have difficulty extending the conversation by making reciprocations related to the topic. Teach children with AS to stay on topic. Initially, have shorter conversations to promote success.

- A child with AS sometimes has a limited range of interests. Try to encourage other interests through positive reinforcement. Praise him or her for trying something new. Keep it brief. Remember, you are not trying to force him or her to like something new but rather to be flexible about trying it.

- Children with AS might exhibit deficits in social language. They might comprehend what is said very literally and might not understand jokes or other figurative types of language (e.g., metaphors, idioms). Use language that is simple and concrete.

- Children with AS might demonstrate a deficit in gross motor skills. Games involving these skills might be difficult, causing anxiety and frustration. As a result, their self-esteem can be low. Keep games fun and simple.

- Children with AS might have difficulty sustaining engagement or focus on a particular task or lesson for an extended amount of time. Timed sessions and lists of tasks/expectations help provide structure and organization.

- Establish a consistent daily routine. This will help the child to understand the expectations and be able to focus on the current activity/task.

- If there are any changes or special events, consider preparing the child beforehand. For example, if there is a school-wide assembly planned, tell the child in advance about this schedule change so that he or she can prepare.

- Children with AS can be very critical of themselves and their faults and weaknesses. It might be difficult for them to handle making mistakes. It is important to teach coping skills for when they are feeling stressed and overwhelmed.

- Although children with AS often have average or above-average intelligence, they sometimes lack higher-level thinking and comprehension skills. Do not assume that everything you say is understood. Additional explanation might be needed.

- Children with AS can be very egocentric. Their perceptions about other people's statements or behaviors can be incorrect. This might cause them to become upset. Help them to comprehend the situation by providing examples and using language that is easy to understand.

- A lot of information on coping with AS is available. Seek help from experts in the field. Continue to learn about AS.